MARVIN REDPOST

SUPER FAST, OUT OF CONTROL!

Louis Sachar
illustrated by Sue Hellard

BLOOMSBURY
CHILDREN'S
BOOKS

To Carla

First published in Great Britain in 2005 by Bloomsbury Publishing Plc,
36 Soho Square, London, W1D 3QY

First published in America in 2000 by Random House, Inc., New York

Text copyright © 2000 by Louis Sachar
Illustrations copyright © 2005 by Sue Hellard
The moral rights of the author and illustrator have been asserted

A CIP record of this book is available from the
British Library

ISBN 978 0 7475 6682 3

Printed in Great Britain by Clays Ltd, St Ives plc

10 9 8 7 6 5 4 3 2

All papers used by Bloomsbury Publishing are natural, recyclable
products made from wood grown in well-managed forests.
The manufacturing processes conform to the environmental
regulations of the country of origin.

Contents

1. Saturday   7

2. Monday   25

3. Tuesday   35

4. Wednesday   51

5. Thursday   61

6. Still Only Thursday   83

7. Saturday   97

8. The Hill   117

9. Monday   127

1
Saturday

Marvin and his friends were hanging out in his backyard.

"What do you want to do?" asked Stuart.

"I dunno," said Marvin.

"It's not fair that your mom won't let us watch TV," griped Nick. "What's so special about fresh air?"

"Let's play unicorns," said Linzy. Linzy was Marvin's five-year-old sister.

"We're not playing unicorns," Marvin grumbled.

"So what do you want to do?" asked Stuart.

"I dunno," said Marvin.

"What about a video game?" asked Nick. "Does that count as TV?"

"I'm the gold unicorn," said Linzy. "Marvin's the rainbow unicorn. Nick, you can be the blue unicorn. Stuart will be the pink unicorn."

"I don't want to be pink," said Stuart. "Why can't I be the gold unicorn?"

"You can't start out being gold," Linzy explained. "First you have to do some good magic. Then the unicorn fairy will turn you into gold."

"We're not playing unicorns," said Marvin.

"How did *you* get to be gold?" asked
Stuart.

"The unicorn fairy made me gold," said
Linzy, "because I used my magic to save
the princess."

"We're not playing unicorns," said Marvin.

"How do you play?" asked Nick.

Linzy stared at Nick. She had never
heard such a dumb question in all

her life. "You
just pretend you're a
unicorn," she said.

"How?" asked Stuart.

Linzy sighed. She couldn't believe
Marvin had such stupid friends.

"Just pretend you're a magical horse
with a horn in your head, like this."

She pranced around the yard, flapping

11

her arms, and sang, "*I'm a unicorn. Yes, I am. I'm a gold unicorn. Yes, I am. Oh, I'm a gold unicorn. Yes, I am.*"

Linzy stopped prancing and flapping. "Your turn, Marvin," she said.

"I don't want to," said Marvin.

"You have to. It's the rules," said Linzy. "Except when I did it, I was gold. You have to be rainbow."

"Just get out of here, Linzy!" snapped Marvin. "Can't you see we're busy! You're such a stupid pest."

Linzy stared hard at Marvin. He was afraid she was going to cry.

"I'm telling the unicorn fairy on you!" she shouted, then stormed into the house. She slammed the door behind her.

Marvin sighed.

"So what do you want to do?" asked Stuart.

"I dunno," said Marvin.

"It's unfair your mom won't let us watch TV," said Nick. "What's wrong with her?"

Marvin shrugged.

"We could ride bikes," suggested Stuart.

Marvin got an uneasy feeling in his stomach. "There's nowhere to go," he said.

"Hey, didn't you get a new mountain bike?" asked Nick.

Marvin felt sick.

"That's right!" said Stuart. "How come you haven't shown it to us?"

Marvin shrugged. "It's just a bike."

"I know!" said Nick. "Let's ride our bikes down Suicide Hill!"

Just hearing those words made Marvin feel like he was falling down a very steep cliff.

Let's ride our bikes down SUICIDE HILL !!!!!!!

"I'll go home and get my bike," said

Stuart. Marvin couldn't believe it. Nick
was a daredevil, but he thought Stuart
was smarter than that.

"I'll bring my stopwatch," said Nick.
"Maybe we can break the record."

"Cool," said Stuart.

Marvin didn't care about breaking records. He was more worried about breaking bones.

Linzy returned to the back door. Marvin was glad to see her. He thought it

might be fun to play unicorns after all.

"Mom wants to see you," Linzy said.

As Marvin walked into the house,
Linzy said, "You're in big trouble now,
mister."

They walked to their mother's office.

Marvin's mother was sitting at her desk, in front of the computer. She worked as an accountant. She helped people figure their taxes. She normally didn't work on Saturdays, but it was getting close to April 15, so she had been very busy lately.

"Did you yell at your sister?" she asked Marvin.

"Kind of," he admitted.

"You need to tell her you're sorry," said his mother.

Marvin turned to Linzy. She was wearing her sad and pitiful face.

He got an idea. "Why should I?" he asked boldly.

"I beg your pardon?" said his mother.

"Linzy is a pest," Marvin said.

"Marvin!" exclaimed his mother.

19

"Now he owes me two sorry's!" said Linzy.

"You're the one who should be sorry," said Marvin. "For being so stupid!"

Marvin's mother looked at him for a long moment. She didn't yell at him. She

simply said, "You need to tell Nick and Stuart it's time for them to go home. Then you will spend the rest of the afternoon in your room."

Marvin pushed his luck. "That's not fair!" he exclaimed. "We were going to ride our bikes down Suicide Hill!"

"You won't be riding your bike for a week," said his mother.

Marvin went back outside and told his friends the bad news.

"Why? What did you do?" asked Stuart.

"Nothing," said Marvin. "My mom's just in a bad mood."

He told them good-bye, then went up to his room. He felt awful. He was glad he wouldn't have to ride down Suicide

Hill, but he felt bad for calling Linzy a stupid pest. More than that, he felt terrible for being so afraid.

He wasn't just afraid of Suicide Hill. He was afraid to ride his new bike.

It seemed so big. And it had hand brakes. He had never used hand brakes before. He also didn't know how to use all the different gears.

What made it worse, he was the one
who had asked for a new bike. He'd
begged for a new bike. His parents had
said it was very expensive. They said he
already had a bicycle, but he'd called that
a "baby bike." He wanted a mountain
bike. He said Linzy could have his old
bike.

And in the end, they bought it for him.

That was ten days ago, and he still hadn't ridden it. Just thinking about it made him sick to his stomach.

At least he wouldn't have to ride it for a week. He wished he still had his baby bike.

2
Monday

"You're so brave," said Casey Happleton. She sat next to Marvin in Mrs. North's class. She had a ponytail that stuck out the side of her head, instead of the back.

Marvin shrugged and smiled. He didn't know why Casey thought he was brave, but he was glad she did.

"Judy and I are going to come watch you," said Casey.

"Watch me what? When?"

"Saturday," said Casey. "When you

ride your new mountain bike down Suicide Hill."

Marvin felt as if he'd been kicked in the stomach. He tried not to show it. He didn't want Casey Happleton to think he was scared. "Who told you that?" he asked.

"Judy," said Casey. "She said you would have ridden down last Saturday, but you got in trouble for calling your sister a stupid pest. Now you can't ride your bike for a week."

Marvin didn't know how Judy Jasper knew so much about his life.

"Stuart told her," said Casey.

Marvin never told Stuart he'd ride down Suicide Hill on Saturday. He just told him that he couldn't ride his bike for a week.

"Marvin," said Mrs. North. "Have you been listening to anything I said?"

He looked at his teacher. "Um, I'm not sure. What did you say?"

Mrs. North gave Marvin the Look.

At recess, Marvin asked Stuart why he told Judy that he had called his sister a stupid pest.

"She asked me," said Stuart.

They were playing wizzle-fish tag.

"Let me get this straight," said Marvin. "Judy Jasper just came up to you and said, 'Did Marvin call his sister a stupid pest?' "

"Something like that," said Stuart.

"And you told her we're going to ride our bikes down Suicide Hill on Saturday?" Marvin asked.

"No," said Stuart.

Marvin was glad about that.

"I told her *you* were going to ride *your* bike down Suicide Hill. My mom won't let me."

"My mom won't let me, either," complained Nick. "Just because it's *dangerous* or something."

30

"But we'll come watch you," said
Stuart.

"You might need someone to call 911,"
said Nick.

Marvin couldn't believe it. They were
the ones who had wanted to ride down
Suicide Hill, not him. He thought he
remembered Nick bragging about how

31

he'd ridden down Suicide Hill lots of times, full speed all the way.

"I thought you said you've ridden down Suicide Hill," he said.

"No, I never said that," said Nick.

Marvin knew he was lying.

He tossed a paper plate on the ground and stepped on it. Everyone had two paper plates. The paper plates were the wizzle fish.

Clarence and
Travis wizzled
beside him.

"Hey, Marvin,"
said Clarence. "Are
you really going to
ride down Suicide Hill?"

"Uh, I'm not sure."

"See, I told you he was chicken!"
Clarence told Travis.

"We're not scared," said Nick.

We? thought Marvin.

"If Marvin says he'll
ride down Suicide
Hill, then he'll
ride down Suicide
Hill," said Stuart.
He patted Marvin
on the back.

33

But Marvin never said he'd ride down Suicide Hill, thought Marvin.

"When?" demanded Clarence.

"Saturday," said Nick. "At twelve o'clock."

"High noon," said Stuart.

"This I've got to see," said Clarence.

"I'm going to get a front-row seat," said Travis.

"It's going to be the biggest wipe-out in history," said Clarence. He and Travis laughed.

Marvin didn't know what to do. Everything was happening too fast. He felt like he was speeding downhill, out of control, unable to stop. He wanted to scream.

3
Tuesday

Linzy was wearing unicorn pajamas. "Do you want to frolic?" she asked.

"Frolic?" asked Marvin. He didn't know what the word meant. He wasn't sure it was a real word.

"That's what unicorns do," Linzy explained. "We frolic."

She showed Marvin how to frolic. She skipped down the hall and sang, "*We're happy, happy unicorns. Oh, happy unicorns frolicking.*"

Marvin didn't feel like frolicking. He wasn't a happy unicorn.

It was Tuesday night. Saturday was only four days away.

He could see the light on in his brother's room. Jacob was doing homework. Jacob had ridden down Suicide Hill before.

Marvin knocked on his brother's door.

"What?"

Jacob sounded annoyed. They gave a lot of homework in middle school.

"I just wanted to ask you something," Marvin said timidly.

"What?" asked Jacob.

Marvin wasn't sure what to ask. "I don't remember," he said.

Jacob glared at him.

Marvin could tell Jacob thought he was

just a dumb little kid. Marvin felt like a
dumb little kid.

He headed back to his room.

The whole school was expecting him to ride down Suicide Hill on Saturday. He couldn't figure out how it happened. He never wanted to ride down Suicide Hill in the first place. It was Stuart and Nick's idea, but their parents wouldn't let them.

That gave him an idea. It was so
obvious, he wondered why he hadn't
thought of it sooner. He walked quickly
to his mother's office.

His mother was working on the
computer. She turned and smiled at
Marvin as he entered.

"Sorry to bother you," Marvin said.

"Oh, that's okay." She took a sip of
coffee.

"In four days I get to ride my bike," Marvin said.

"That's right," said his mother. "I hope you've learned your lesson."

Marvin nodded. "You know the first place I'm going to ride it?" he asked, trying to sound excited.

His mother smiled and asked, "Where?"

"Suicide Hill!"

"Sounds exciting," said his mother. She entered some numbers into the computer.

Marvin thought maybe she hadn't heard him. Or maybe she thought it was

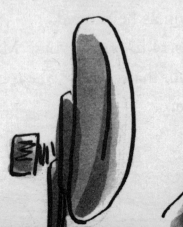

no big deal, since Jacob had ridden down
it lots of times. Didn't she realize Jacob
was a lot older?

"*Suicide* Hill," he repeated. "I'm going
to ride my brand-new expensive bike
super fast down Suicide Hill!"

"I'm glad to see you're so excited about riding your new bike. Your father and I were beginning to wonder."

"Stuart's and Nick's parents won't let them ride their bikes down Suicide Hill," said Marvin. "I guess they think it's dangerous or something. For a *third grader*."

"I guess," said his mother. She entered some more numbers into the computer.

Marvin wondered if she heard anything he said. He kept trying. "I guess Stuart's mom is worried he might break his arm, or worse."

"I know you'll be careful," said his mother.

"Sure, I'll try to be careful," said Marvin. "But when you're going downhill super fast, out of control, it's—"

"Is it raining?" asked his mother.

Marvin didn't know what that had to do with anything. "I don't think so," he said, but then he saw a flash of lightning.

A few seconds later, he heard thunder. A few seconds after that, Linzy came running into the room.

"Turn off the computer!" she screamed. She was wearing her wild and worried face. She clutched her mother.

"There's nothing to worry about," said her mother.

There was another flash of lightning.

"Turn it off! Turn it off!" Linzy demanded. She was crying.

"I know you're scared," said her mother. "But I—"

"The lightning will come through the computer!" Linzy shrieked.

44

Her mother sighed. "We are all very safe," she said.

Marvin's father came into the study. He picked up Linzy and held her close. "Everything is all right," he told her.

"She has to turn it off before it explodes."

"She has an important job to do. And it's our job to let her do it. You too, Marvin."

Marvin followed his father as he carried Linzy to her room and set her on her bed.

"Can I sleep with you, Marvin?" Linzy asked. "Please?"

Marvin felt bad for her, but he'd tried sleeping with Linzy once before. She could never keep still. She kept kicking him all night, and ended up sleeping sideways across the bed.

"Lightning and thunder are just part of nature," he said.

"The bad part," said Linzy.

"You are perfectly safe," said her father. "Do you think I would leave you alone if I thought you were in danger?"

"No," Linzy whimpered.

"You're the gold unicorn," said Marvin. "Unicorns aren't afraid of storms."

There was a loud clap of thunder, and she ducked under the covers.

"You know the thunder can't hurt you," said her father.

"I know," Linzy said, from under the covers.

"But you're still scared?" asked her father.

"Yes."

"Try to be brave," said her father. "Remember, the fear isn't on the outside. The fear is inside your head."

Linzy's head came out from under the covers. She looked puzzled, as if she was trying to figure out what that meant.

Marvin tried to figure it out, too.

"You need to stand up to that storm," said her father. "And say, 'I'm not afraid of you!' "

Linzy gave it a try. She sat up straight in her bed and looked out the window. "I'm not afraid of you!" she declared.

"Good," said her father. "That's my brave girl." He kissed her good night, then started out the door. "C'mon, Marvin."

Marvin could see Linzy trembling with fear. As he walked out the door, he heard

her whisper to herself, "I'm a gold
unicorn. Yes, I am. Oh, I'm a very brave
unicorn. Yes, I am."

4
Wednesday

Marvin knew what he had to do. He just had to stand up to Suicide Hill and say, "I'm not afraid of you!"

It was like his father had said. The fear was all inside his head. There was nothing on the outside that was scary. His mother would never let him ride down Suicide Hill if it was really dangerous. Would she?

Jacob had gone down Suicide Hill lots of times. If Jacob could do it, so could he.

"Keep your tongue inside your mouth," said Casey Happleton.

Marvin was eating lunch. He thought his tongue *was* inside his mouth.

"My brother's friend knows someone who bit off the tip of his tongue while riding down Suicide Hill," said Casey.

Marvin touched the tip of his tongue to his teeth.

"It wasn't even a wipe-out," said Casey. "He was going down Suicide Hill real fast, and the tip of his tongue was sticking out of his mouth, like this."

Casey held her fists out in front of her, like she was gripping handlebars. She looked like she was concentrating really hard. Her tongue stuck out of her mouth.

Everybody else at the table laughed, but

Marvin didn't see anything funny about it.

"Then his bike hit just a tiny little ittybitty rock," said Casey, "and he bit it off. He didn't even know he did it until he got to the bottom of the hill and tried to talk."

Casey did an impersonation of someone trying to talk without a tongue. Again,

everyone except Marvin laughed.

"What happened to his tongue?" asked
Stuart.

"No one knows," said Casey. "They
had a whole huge search party out to
look for it, but no one ever found it. It's
still up there, somewhere."

"Maybe Marvin will find it," said Judy.

Marvin shrugged. His mouth was closed tight. His tongue was safely on the inside.

"Be sure your shoelaces are tied real good," warned Kenny. "My cousin knows someone whose shoelace got wrapped around his bike pedal. He was riding his bike real fast, and every time the pedal went around, it made his shoe tighter ... and tighter ... and tighter ... and tighter ... and tighter. There was nothing he could do. He was going too fast to stop."

"What happened?" asked Nick.

"It strangled his foot. He lost two toes."

"How?" asked Casey. "What'd they do, pop off his foot?"

"I don't know how it happened," said Kenny. "I wasn't there. Somebody told my

cousin about it, and my cousin doesn't
lie."

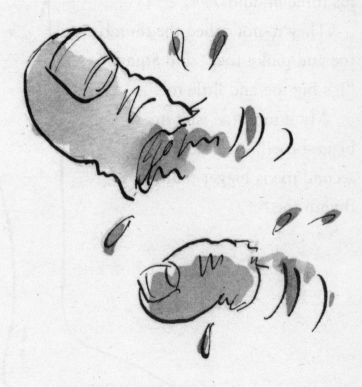

"Which toes did he lose?"
asked Judy.

"The thumb-toe and the
pinky-toe, I think. He still has
his three middle ones."

"They're not called the thumb-
toe and pinky-toe," said Stuart.
"It's big toe and little toe."

"My thumb-toe isn't my
biggest toe," said Melanie. "My
second toe is bigger than my
thumb-toe."

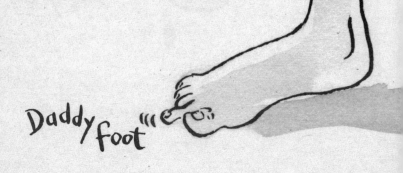

Daddy foot

"My toes are different on each foot," said Judy Jasper.

Judy took off her shoes and socks. She explained that her parents' feet were different. On her mother's feet, the thumb-toe was the biggest. On her father's feet, the second toe was the biggest.

Judy showed everyone her feet. On her left foot, her thumb-toe was the biggest. On

Mommy foot

her right foot, the second toe was the biggest. "I call this one my mommy foot, and this one my daddy foot," she said.

Nick stared at Judy's feet. "That's the most amazing thing I've ever seen in my whole life," he said.

Marvin didn't even look at Judy's amazing feet. He was thinking about how often his shoelaces came untied, even when they were double-knotted.

The lunch teacher, Mrs. Grant, came by and made Judy put her shoes and socks back on.

5
Thursday

A policewoman came to Marvin's classroom. She wore a blue police uniform and a silver badge. Handcuffs dangled from her belt. She didn't have a gun. Her hair was red, like Marvin's, and almost as short.

"This is Officer Watson," said Mrs. North. "She wants to talk to us about something important, and she's also brought some interesting things to share with us."

Marvin wondered if she was there to tell him not to ride down Suicide Hill. He hoped so.

Officer Watson said hello to the class. The first thing she showed them was a bulletproof vest. She put it on over her police uniform. Then she took it off and passed it around the room.

Marvin was surprised by how heavy it was. Officer Watson must be really strong, he realized, to wear it. He wished he could borrow it when he rode down Suicide Hill. *If* he rode down Suicide Hill.

"Are those real handcuffs?" asked Nick.

Officer Watson turned to Mrs. North

and asked, "Aren't they supposed to raise their hands before asking a question?"

"They're supposed to," said Mrs. North.

Officer Watson wiggled her finger at Nick, asking for him to come up to the front of the room.

Marvin watched Nick nervously get out of his chair and go to her.

"Hold out your hand," she told him.

Nick held out his hand.

Officer Watson took the handcuffs off her belt. She clasped one of the cuffs around Nick's wrist.

Everyone laughed.

Then she walked him over to Mrs. North. She clasped the other cuff around Mrs. North's wrist.

Marvin gasped. Next to him, Casey

Happleton laughed so hard her ponytail went around in circles.

"Yes, those are real handcuffs," Officer Watson told Nick.

Marvin had never seen Nick's face so red.

Officer Watson patted her pockets. "What did I do with the key?" she asked. She looked worried.

So did Nick.

But she was only kidding. She unlocked the handcuffs, and Nick ran back to his seat.

She also brought a fingerprint kit. She had everyone press their thumbs on an ink pad and put their thumbprints on a piece of paper.

The whole class had purple thumbs.

The last thing Officer Watson showed them was a lie detector.

"I bet Mrs. North would love to have that!" said Travis.

"I don't need one," said Mrs. North. "I always know when one of my students isn't telling the truth. That's the first thing you learn when you become a teacher."

"Who would like to try it out?" asked Officer Watson.

Marvin had an awful feeling in the pit of his stomach. He *knew* Officer Watson was going to call on him and ask him if he was scared to ride his bike.

He ducked his head down and tried to hide behind Warren, the boy who sat in front of him. He felt like a criminal.

Officer Watson seemed to be looking right at him. "How about you?" she asked.

"Okay," said Casey Happleton. She hopped out of her seat. Marvin watched her sideways ponytail bob up and down as she went to the front of the room.

The lie detector was on Mrs. North's desk. Casey sat in Mrs. North's chair. Officer Watson attached some wires to

Casey's right arm and fingers. She strapped a belt around her chest.

"I'm going to ask you some questions," Officer Watson told Casey. "This machine will let me know if you are lying. Ready?"

"Ready," said Casey.

"What's your name?"

"Michael Jordan," said Casey.

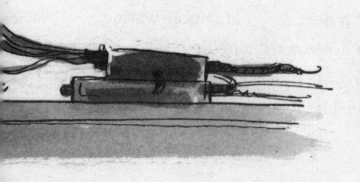

Officer Watson checked the machine. "That was not the truth," she said.

"Casey Happleton," said Casey.

"How old are you?"

"Nine."

"What did you have for breakfast this morning?"

"Scrambled eggs."

"I don't think that's the truth," said Officer Watson.

Casey sighed. "Well, my mom gave me scrambled eggs, but I fed them to my dog."

"How does that machine know what Casey had for breakfast?" asked Clarence.

"It doesn't," said Officer Watson. "When you tell a lie, your body gets nervous. Your muscles tense. You sweat a little bit more, and there are changes in

your heartbeat and breathing. The
machine registers those changes in your
body."

She asked Casey some more questions.

"Did you do all your homework yesterday?"

"Yes."

"Did anyone help you?"

"No."

Officer Watson cleared her throat. "Are you sure?"

Casey frowned. "My mom helped me."

"That's better," said Officer Watson.

"There's nothing wrong with that," said Mrs. North.

"Do you like Mrs. North?" asked Officer Watson.

"Hey!" Casey exclaimed. "That's not a fair question."

"Okay, I'll ask a different question."

"Ask her if she likes Marvin Redpost!" called Melanie.

Officer Watson smiled. "Who's Marvin Redpost?"

Everyone pointed at Marvin.

Officer Watson turned back to Casey. "Do you like Marvin Redpost?"

Marvin buried his head under his arms.
But he didn't cover his ears. For a long
time Casey didn't answer. Then she said,
"I like Mrs. North."

Officer Watson unhooked her and let
her return to her seat.

"Okay, we've had some fun," Officer

Watson told the class. "But now I want everyone to settle down. I want to talk to you about something important. It may save your life."

Marvin paid close attention.

"I'm talking about illegal drugs," said Officer Watson.

She told the class that drugs were bad for them. Drugs could kill you. Drugs could destroy your brain and make you stupid. If you started doing drugs, even just once, you might not be able to stop.

Everybody promised Officer Watson they would never take illegal drugs.

She walked around the room and in between the desks. She stopped next to Kenny. "What if all your friends took drugs?" she asked him. "Then would you?"

"No way!" said Kenny.

She turned to Nick. "What if they said they wouldn't be friends unless you took drugs?"

"Then they're not really my friends," said Nick.

"If my friend jumped off the Empire State Building, that doesn't mean I should jump off, too," said Judy.

"If they were my friends," said Casey Happleton, "I would do everything I could to get them to stop using drugs."

"Very good," said Officer Watson. She leaned on Marvin's desk and stared right

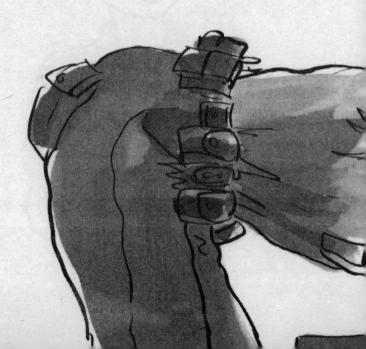

into his eyes. "What about you, Marvin?" she asked. "What if everyone said, 'Marvin Redpost is chicken!'?"

She made him feel nervous. "I—I still w-wouldn't," he said.

"Good for you," she said. "That's not being scared. That's being smart. Remember, taking drugs doesn't make

you brave. It takes a lot more courage,
sometimes, to say no to your friends."

Marvin nodded. His hands were
sweaty. His body was tense. His heart was
beating a little faster than normal. He
took a deep breath.

6
Still Only Thursday

Marvin sat on a stool in the kitchen. He stared at the wall. He'd been sitting that way ever since he got home from school.

He didn't know what he was supposed to do. Should he look his fear in the eye and ride down Suicide Hill? Or was that stupid, like taking drugs? Officer Watson had said that sometimes the bravest thing you can do is say no to your friends.

He knew his friends wouldn't think he was being brave. They'd think he was scared.

And they'd be right. He was scared of Suicide Hill. But maybe he was smart to be scared.

His father had told Linzy she had to stand up to her fears. But Suicide Hill was different than thunder and lightning. He could get hurt going down Suicide Hill. Thunder and lightning couldn't hurt Linzy.

No, that wasn't true either, he realized.
Maybe thunder couldn't hurt her, but if
she got struck by lightning, it could kill
her. Maybe Linzy was right. Maybe
lightning could come through the
computer.

Going down Suicide Hill wasn't as bad
as being struck by lightning. He didn't
think he'd be killed going down Suicide
Hill. Maybe just break an arm and a leg.

Other kids have ridden down Suicide Hill, he reminded himself. *They didn't get hurt.*

So? Other kids have taken drugs, too. Just because other kids do something, that doesn't mean you should, too. If your friends jump off the Empire State Building, that doesn't mean you should, too.

But Nick and Stuart weren't even jumping off the Empire State Building. They just expected him to jump.

Maybe his friends had forgotten all about Suicide Hill. Nobody mentioned it once today at school. All anyone talked about was Officer Watson and the lie detector.

He never felt more confused in his life. He wished he could practice riding his

bike. He needed to see how the brakes
and gears worked.

He remembered the man at the bike
shop telling him never to use just the
front brake. He was supposed to use the
back brake, or both brakes together. If he

tried to stop using just the front brake, the bike might flip over on his head.

The front door opened. "Hey, Mar," said Jacob.

"Hiya, Marvin," said Nate. Nate was Jacob's best friend.

They threw their backpacks on the counter and attacked the refrigerator.

"I hear you're going to ride down Suicide Hill," said Nate.

"Uh, maybe," said Marvin.

"You better not wimp out," said Nate. "Some of the guys at school said you were a baby, but I stuck up for you. Now my reputation is on the line."

Marvin didn't say anything. He couldn't believe middle school kids had been talking about him, a puny third grader.

"Can I ask you a question?" he asked his brother.

"Sure," said Jacob, his mouth full of cookies and pickles.

"How do you know which is front and which is back?"

"What?" asked Jacob.

"Well, I haven't really ridden my bike a whole lot. How do you know which brake is for the front tire, and which one is for the back tire?"

Jacob thought a moment as he swallowed a mouthful of food. "Right is back, left is front," he said. "No, wait. Right is front, left is back. No, I think I

was right the first time. Left is front—"

"Left is back, right is front," said Nate.

"No, right is back, left is front," said
Jacob.

"You sure?" asked Nate.

"I think so," said Jacob.

It always took Marvin a moment to

figure out his left from his right.
He knew he wouldn't have time if he was
speeding down Suicide Hill.

"I really don't think about it when I'm
on my bike," said Nate. "It just comes
natural."

"You don't want to brake just with
your front brake," said Jacob. "Your bike
could flip over."

Marvin nodded. He'd heard that
before.

"Suicide Hill is so steep, you should probably use both brakes all the time," said Nate.

"What about gears?" Marvin asked.

"What about them?" asked Nate.

"Do I need to shift gears? Which gear should I use?"

"High gear," said Jacob.

"Low gear," said Nate, at almost the same time.

"Low gear going up, high gear going down," said Jacob.

"I thought it was high gear going up, and low gear going down," said Nate.

"No, low up, high down," said Jacob.

"I don't really think about it when I'm on my bike," said Nate. "It just comes natural."

Marvin didn't think it would come natural to him.

"You won't need to worry about gears going down the hill," said Jacob. "You'll coast almost the whole way. But remember to lean into the turns."

Marvin didn't know what that meant.

"You have to lean your bike way over on the sharp turns," Nate explained.

"Have you ever watched a motorcycle race? They lean way over the whole time."

Marvin had never seen a motorcycle race. He didn't want to do any fancy riding. He just wanted to get down the hill alive. "I'm just going to try to keep my bike straight up," he said.

"You can't do that," said Jacob. "You have to lean into the turns. Otherwise you'll slide off the path and you'll go over the cliff."

"It comes natural," Nate assured him.

Jacob and Nate went on up to Jacob's room.

Marvin stayed where he was, staring at the wall. *Well, it's only Thursday*, he told himself.

He still had two whole days.

7

Saturday

Marvin couldn't believe it was already Saturday. What happened to Friday? The week had sped by super fast, out of control.

He walked out through the laundry room into the garage. His shoes were double-knotted. So was his stomach.

His bike was leaning against the side wall. It had been leaning there for almost three weeks. "Don't you want to try it out?" his father had asked when they first brought it home from the bike shop.

"I'm kind of tired," Marvin had said.

Now he took hold of the handlebars. "I'm not afraid of you," he whispered. He slowly rolled the bike backward, between the van and the garbage pail. The pedal

banged against his shin as he made his way out of the garage and onto the driveway.

He still hadn't decided if he would go down Suicide Hill, but he had to go at least as far as Stuart's house. It was decided that he and Nick would meet at Stuart's, and then they'd all ride to Suicide Hill together.

Nick and Stuart were the ones who decided this. It seemed to Marvin that he didn't make any of his own decisions anymore. His life was being decided by others.

His bike helmet dangled off the end of one handlebar. He put it on, but it didn't seem to fit right. The strap was too tight under his chin, and the helmet seemed way too loose at the top of his head. He

hoped he hadn't put it on backward.

He stared at his giant bicycle. His
parents had chosen a bicycle that was a
little big for him. "You'll grow into it,"
his father had said. "We don't want to
have to buy another bike in six months."

He had to lean it way over to try and get his leg over it. It was impossible. As he tried to lift himself onto the seat, the bike almost fell. He just managed to stick his foot out and catch himself.

He tried several more times, hopping on one foot and scraping his leg against the pedal. He couldn't do it.

How am I supposed to ride down Suicide Hill if I can't even get on my bike? he wondered.

He thought about all the kids waiting for him at Suicide Hill. Casey and Judy. Clarence and Travis. Nate and all the kids from middle school.

Marvin walked the bike down the driveway and into the street. He edged it next to the curb and then rotated the pedals into position. Then, standing on the curb, he was able to stretch his leg over the top of the bike and just barely touch the pedal on the other side.

He hopped on. The bike wobbled. The tire rubbed against the curb and he almost fell, but he managed to turn the handlebars and straighten out. He pedaled hard. He felt himself gain his balance. He headed toward Stuart's house.

Now that Marvin was on the bike, it felt almost the same as his old bike. He was just higher off the ground. He didn't try to shift gears. And he hoped he wouldn't have to use the brakes.

There was only one corner between his

house and Stuart's. He took it nice and slow, almost too slow. He found it easier to keep his balance when he was going a little faster, but if he went too fast, he might have to use his brakes.

Stuart's driveway was uphill. It slowed him down enough that he didn't have to use his brakes. He let the bike roll to a stop, then hopped off. He let it fall beside him.

He knocked on Stuart's door. As he

waited for someone to answer it, he
looked back at his bike. He hoped he'd be
able to get back on it without too much
trouble.

Stuart's mother opened the door and
said, "Hi, Marvin. Come on in. The boys
are watching a movie."

Marvin walked through the kitchen and
into the family room. His friends were
lying on the floor, staring at the TV.
Before he could say anything, Nick said,

"Shush! It's the good part."

"It's almost twelve o'clock," said Marvin. "We have to get going."

"After the movie," said Stuart.

Marvin couldn't believe it. "How long will that be?" he asked.

"I don't know," said Stuart.

"Shush!" said Nick.

"Can't you watch it later?" Marvin asked.

"You look funny in that helmet," said Stuart.

"Do you think it's on backward?" Marvin asked.

Stuart didn't answer. He was staring back at the TV set.

"It's a video," Marvin pointed out. "You can watch it later."

"We want to watch it now," said Nick. "Besides, we haven't had lunch yet."

"Lunch!" exclaimed Marvin. "Everyone is waiting for me at Suicide Hill."

"Then go," said Stuart. "I still have to eat lunch."

"Ooh, did you see that?" asked Nick.

"Gross!" said Stuart.

Marvin didn't know what to do. He didn't want to have to go to Suicide Hill alone. He didn't even know if he was allowed to ride there alone.

He was allowed to ride to Stuart's house, because it was just around the block. Suicide Hill was much farther away.

He decided to call home. If his mother wouldn't let him go, then there was nothing he could do about it. No one could blame him. It would be her fault. And Stuart and Nick's.

He used the kitchen phone. His father was the one who answered. Marvin explained the problem.

"I think it will be fine," his father said. "There are no busy streets along the way. And I appreciate the fact that you called. It shows you're responsible. If you didn't call, I wouldn't have let you go."

Marvin hung up. He tried to make sense of what his father said. If he didn't call, how could his father have said he couldn't go?

He wished he'd talked to his mother instead. She never would have let him go.

"Well, I'm going," he told Nick and Stuart. "So long."

They stared at the TV.

He went back outside. He picked up his bike and walked it down the driveway.

He wasn't sure he'd ride down Suicide Hill, but at least he had to go there. He couldn't leave everybody waiting. He had

to be brave enough to tell them he was
scared.

He set his bike next to the curb. He put his foot on the pedal and quickly hoisted his other leg over. He was up and pedaling before he had time to worry about it.

He rode quickly, afraid that he was already late. He turned right off Stuart's street, rode past two more streets, then turned left on the road that led to Suicide Hill.

The road was uphill the whole way. It became harder and harder to pedal. He wondered if he should try shifting gears.

He had two gear shifts, one on either end of his handlebars. The one on his left was numbered 1 to 3. The arrow was in the middle, at 2. The one on his right was numbered 1 to 7. The arrow pointed to 5. He took a chance. He rotated the right

gear shift one notch, so that the arrow
pointed to **6**.

Suddenly it became almost impossible
to pedal. His bike slowed to a stop, and
he had to put his foot down to keep from
falling.

He caught his breath. He knew he should never have tried shifting gears. He promised himself never to do that again.

He walked his bike to the curb and hopped back on. But once again, he couldn't pedal, and he fell off to the side.

It was impossible. The bike was in the wrong gear, and he couldn't shift gears until the bike was moving. But how could he get it moving if it was in the wrong gear?

He wondered if the kids at Suicide Hill were getting impatient. He could imagine some of the middle schoolers telling Nate, "See, I told you Marvin Redpost was a wimp."

He turned the bike around and pointed it downhill. He didn't bother taking it to the curb. He just stepped on the pedal

and threw his other leg over as he rolled down the hill.

The bike wasn't really *that* big.

He shifted the gear back to **5**. Then he shifted one notch further, to **4**.

He made a U-turn and continued up the hill. It was a lot easier to pedal now that he was in a lower gear. He shifted to **3**. Even better.

He had to keep on shifting gears as he continued following the road higher and higher. After a while both gears were pointed at **1**, and it was still hard to pedal.

Ahead of him, the road made a sharp turn to the left. A steel barrier prevented cars from going straight.

But Marvin wasn't in a car. Using his right-hand brake, he stopped his bike. He got off and walked around the barrier. He took several long, deep breaths, then looked over the edge of Suicide Hill.

8
The Hill

Where was everybody? Marvin wondered
if maybe they all got tired of waiting and
went home. Or they could be waiting at
the bottom of the hill. After all, why
should *they* struggle to get to the top?

"Hello!" he shouted. "I'm here!"

There was no answer.

He couldn't see the bottom of the hill.
His eyes followed a dirt path that
zigzagged through some rocks, then
disappeared behind a large bush. He

couldn't see anything beyond that.

"Anyone down there?" he called.

A van stopped on the other side of the barrier. Marvin turned around to see his mother. She got out of the van and stepped over the barrier. "Since Nick and

Stuart weren't riding with you, I thought I'd better make sure you were all right."

Marvin was glad to see her.

"I dropped Jacob, Linzy, and your dad at the bottom of the hill," she said. "They wanted to see you come down."

"Was anyone else there?" asked Marvin.

"No."

"You sure?" Marvin asked.

"I didn't see anybody."

"Do you know what time it is?"

His mother checked her watch. "A couple of minutes after twelve."

"What about Nate?" Marvin asked. "Did he come with Jacob?"

"No."

Marvin couldn't believe it. Although, now that he thought about it, Nate had

never said he was coming. And none of
Marvin's classmates had talked about
Suicide Hill since that day at lunch. When
was that? Wednesday? Three days ago.

He shook his head and smiled. He had

been so worried about what everybody else thought. But nobody else really cared.

"So *this* is Suicide Hill," said his mother, peering over the edge.

Marvin nodded.

"It's steep, isn't it?"

Marvin nodded again.

"You sure this is something you want to do?" she asked. "You don't have to if you don't want to."

"I know," said Marvin.

He looked back down the hill. He wrapped his fingers around the handlebars. The bike felt sturdy. Not like his old baby bike. This bike was made for this hill.

"I want to," he said.

It felt good to make his own decision. Not for anyone else. For himself.

He looked back down the hill and whispered, "Oh, I'm a very brave unicorn. Yes, I am." Then he stepped up on the pedal and swung his leg over the other side.

He shifted the gears as he watched the front tire slowly roll over the edge. The trail was narrow and steep. He squeezed

both brakes as he tried to stay in the
middle of the dirt path. He went between
a couple of jagged boulders, then around
a large bush. His tires skidded from side
to side.

At last he came to a place where the
trail was straight, so he eased off the
brakes. That was a mistake.

The next thing he knew, he was speeding toward a cliff. He gripped the brakes hard and turned sharply. The wheels skidded inches from the cliff. He had to jerk the bike back the other way to avoid a sharp-edged boulder—once again he was heading toward the cliff. Gripping the brakes with all his might, he leaned into the turn.

The trail then widened and got easier. He caught his breath. He came to a point where he went uphill for a short distance and needed to pedal. He shifted to a lower gear.

Then the trail turned back downhill. He went through a series of wide, smooth turns that were fast and fun.

It kind of looked like this.

As Marvin made the last turn, he could

see the bottom of the hill. The rest of the
way was very steep, but straight. Then it
opened up into a wide, flat area. He let go
of the brakes and went full speed.

As he streaked down the hill, he saw his family waving their arms and cheering for him. His father did one of his real loud whistles.

"Way to go, Mar!" Jacob called as Marvin went flying past him.

He made a U-turn and brought his bike to a halt next to Linzy.

"You're a gold unicorn now," she told him.

Marvin smiled. His heart was beating super fast, out of control.

9
Monday

Nobody asked Marvin about Suicide Hill.
Marvin didn't tell anybody.

Only one person cared whether or not
Marvin Redpost rode his bike down
Suicide Hill. That person was Marvin
Redpost.

About the Author

Louis Sachar lives in Austin, Texas. His wife, Carla, is the bike rider of the family. She rides for miles every day, super fast, up and down the steep hills of Austin. Louis sometimes rides with her but has trouble keeping up. He prefers to get his exercise by jogging with his two dogs, Lucky and Tippy.